The Remarkable Insight Of Jellybeans *and* Understanding

AMY LAURENS

OTHER WORKS

SANCTUARY SERIES

Where Shadows Rise
Through Roads Between
When Worlds Collide

KADITEOS SERIES

How Not To Acquire A Castle

STORM FOXES SERIES

A Fox of Storms and Starlight

SHORTER WORKS

Bones Of The Sea
Darkness And Good
Dreaming Of Forests
It All Changes Now
Rush Job
Trust Issues

NON-FICTION

How To Write Dogs
How To Theme
How To Create Cultures
How To Create Life
How To Map
The 32 Worst Mistakes People Make About Dogs

Find other works by the author at
www.amylaurens.com

The Remarkable Insight Of

Jellybeans *and* Understanding

INKLET #67

AMY LAURENS

www.inkprintpress.com

Print ISBN: 978-1-925825-69-5
eBook ISBN: 9798201525224

www.inkprintpress.com

National Library of Australia Cataloguing-in-Publication Data
Laurens, Amy 1985 –
The Remarkable Insight Of Jellybeans and
Understanding
40 p.
ISBN: 978-1-925825-69-5
Inkprint Press, Canberra, Australia
1. Fiction—Family Life—Marriage & Divorce 2. Fiction-
Women 3. Fiction—Literary. 4.. Fiction—Short Stories

First Print Edition: October 2021
Cover design © Inkprint Press
Interior art © Amy Laurens

THE REMARKABLE INSIGHT OF JELLYBEANS

THEY SIT ON THE LOUNGE THEY BOUGHT together, curled up in opposite ends while the TV blares. He sounds like the TV, droning on, talking with monotonous fervour about his job, his friends, his bike—and she can't make herself care. It's like ads, like prime time, like seeing the same reruns month after month after month, and what was clever and funny once is now mundane. It makes her think of canned laughter and dishes, taking out the garbage and catching buses. Forever, it's been like this; he talks, she listens, never interrupting, never interjecting, the perfect girlfriend, the perfect listener, perfectly selfless, an empty vessel just waiting to be filled— and he's never asked about her day, not once.

He pauses for a breath and, carefully, she lifts the jellybean jar from where it has been resting against her tucked-up ankles, out of sight but not out of mind, cool glass pressing against bare skin, ice in a beige desert storm. She unscrews it with perfect, measured movements, not too quick, not too loud, not wanting to interrupt his train of thought.

He glances over. "Can I have some?"

He hadn't wanted her to buy them, called them a frivolous waste of money, and as soon as she got them home she felt like he was right; jellybeans had no place in their pantry, nowhere to sit that didn't highlight their out-of-placeness, garish in the cool dim company of potatoes and garlic, practical tinned tomatoes and stockpiles of penne pasta. He hadn't wanted her to buy them, but she'd known all along he'd finish most of them, because that's just how it was, and she'd never interrupted.

"Sure." She peers down at a jar full of sugar, bright colour and empty calories, flavour that kisses the tongue then vanishes, leaving the mouth cloyed with generic sweetness. Bright colours, like fruit, or hummingbirds, or hope.

She chooses a dark brown one speckled with white, then twists around, arm extended so she can pop it into his mouth, a sugar pill, a placebo. His tongue brushes her fingertips, bird-like, here-and-then-gone, and she returns her fingers to her lap and rubs them on her skirt.

"Yuck," he says, screwing up his nose, eyes never leaving the TV. "I hate the coffee ones."

"Sorry," she says, and fishes a second bean from the jar, brown, with white speckles. "Another?"

He nods, and stares glazedly at the telly; he has exhausted his supply of conversation topics, and she is unsurprised, because every night they are the same, and they are limited, and they are never hers, like the books kept on display to impress the neighbours or the ornaments that line the hallway. She presses the jellybean against his lips, a tiny act of rebellion, and he takes it without looking, and again she scrubs her fingers on her skirt.

He makes a face and spits out something that was perfect once, but is now half-chewed and mangled, its clear, worthless centre exposed: a shot of glucose, an empty hope, a painted, hollow corpse. "I just said I don't like the coffee ones," he snaps, shooting a sideways glare into her temple where it pierces, lodges, and she can almost feel the blood trickling down.

"Sorry!" she says defensively, resisting the need to rub her temple. "I didn't mean it." But a thrill stirs inside her stomach. He'll believe her, of course he will, because she never interrupts—but this time, she meant it, and she hears alarums sound and horses neigh, and the clash of sword on shield.

"Hmph." He reaches into the jar and scoops out his own handful, multi-coloured like the eggs of a rainbow, then scoffs them down all at once, chewing indiscriminately.

What's the point? she wonders. Why have different flavours in the first place, if you won't stop to savour them?

She closes her eyes and selects one bean, just one, its sugary surface smooth and slightly sticky. Without opening her eyes, she places it delicately on her tongue, closes her mouth around it like a secret, sucks it close and concentrates. Sharp, sweet but acid, tart—not lemon, but something close.

Grapefruit, she decides, and rolls it between her teeth, trying to make the flavour last—but of course, the flavour's gone and she's left with that same inevitable, generic sweetness.

She feels the same; just a generic sort of sweet, a hollow-caloried person-shaped lump, valueless, worthless but for fleeting gratification that weighs heavy afterwards on the tongue. Does he feel that way about her? Although she listens, does it satisfy him? After the first flavour of their relationship is gone, is she still enough?

She watches as he grabs another handful of jellybeans and sucks them down, swallowing them like liquid, concentration on the sitcom never faltering. Yes. He is satisfied with bright colours that smack of hope. Empty nutrients comfort him.

She remembers the man she saw earlier this evening, dark and tall, striding between the rows of the fruit market with confidence like a million-dollar cruiser amidst dinghies. He'd confronted a seller over her bruised nectarines, their blushing skins marred by brown stains of abuse. He'd caressed ripe lady fingers, inhaled sour green mangoes, savoured a dark burgundy grape. Not everyone is satisfied by hollowness, she realises.

She is not satisfied.

He shifts beside her, mindless, and she knows that any moment now he will ask for his nightly cup of coffee—supermarket coffee, over-roasted coffee, old and dull and cheap coffee. But she is sick of crappy coffee; it reminds her of days spent under the flickering eye of fluorescent light bulbs, walled in by partitions covered with geometric patterns in sensible colours meant to detract from the fact that really, they are padded.

A shiver touches her spine and she stares at the jellybeans, wondering.

And of course, "Coffee?" he says, and she wraps her fingers around the neck of the jar and decides. Generic sweetness is not inevitable. "No," she says as her heart tries to break open her rib cage, or burst her veins with blood flow. She touches her fingertips to her temple.

He tears himself away from cued laughter and crude humour to give her an incredulous stare. "What do you mean?"

She shakes her head, lips sealed against the weight of what she has said. She can't repeat it, it's too heavy, it will break her jaw with its passing— but she has said it once, and maybe once will be enough.

He raises an eyebrow. "Bad day at work?"

And there it is, the very thing she's been waiting for all these months, the thing she thought she needed to hear—only now, she realises it's not enough. It's jellybeans, with the gloss of hope hiding emptiness inside, and he, who is satisfied with handfuls of sugar and cheap, dirty coffee, will never be enough.

She thinks again of the man in the markets, of sun-ripened strawberries made sweet with heat, of apples crisp and fresh so the juice runs down her chin when she bites into them, and she turns to him with eyes full of tears, with hands full of jellybeans, and a heart full of fruit. "I'm sorry," she says, and catches his arm before he can turn away, before he can dismiss her words as platitudes. "I can't stay here," she whispers, begging him to understand and knowing perfectly well that candy and cost-saving never can. "I'm leaving. I'm sorry," and she's not.

While he sits there in stunned silence, she passes him the jellybean jar and stands. "You'll be fine," she says, and smiles. "What we have is replaceable."

Gaping, he watches as she walks to the bedroom, where she picks up her blackwood jewellery box that holds the antique necklace she asked her grandma for when she was twelve, empties the single drawer in the dresser that holds all the clothes she's ever chosen for herself, slips on her favourite shoes and rummages in the depths of the wardrobe for the pale blue, fake-crocodile handbag she'd fallen in love with at the county show, the one he hated so much she'd never dared use.

It smells of feet and old carpet, pencils and overripe bananas. A smile spreads across her face as she gathers up all the decisions she's ever made, and carries them to her car.

"I'm sorry," she says as he stands on the porch, still speechless.

But she's not, and she drives away with the satisfying sweetness of mangoes on her tongue.

THE MAKING OF
THE REMARKABLE INSIGHT OF JELLYBEANS

I don't remember much about the writing of Jellybeans, except that I was not far past university, or perhaps still at university, and Costco had just opened—an imported Americanism, a novelty in our Australian city. It's out by the airport, just as huge and super-sized as I imagine it must be in America—and in one of our first visits, my husband and I treated ourselves to a giant plastic jar of Jellybelly jellybeans.

Actually, I do remember now: this was post-university, in my first year of teaching, because I still remember us curling up on the lounge together after dinner, watching TV and eating an inordinate amount of jellybeans simply because we could. The warm glow of the house's golden tones, the leather of the lounge that always sticks just that little tiny bit and protests loudly when you move, the flickering TV, the smell of sugar, sticky fingers, the feel of someone's tongue tip against your fingertips…

Luckily, however, I never lived anything else of the story, and I remain happily married to my husband. But respect to the woman of this story, for realising that she was worth more, for standing up for herself, and for leaving to find a better dream.

UNDERSTANDING

Walking into the house again after five years, it still smells exactly the same. You still use that lemon and vanilla brew on the stove to freshen the kitchen, still use the same brand of shoe wax on Dad's boots in the hallway. And underneath it all, I can still smell the Windex.

Windex and vanilla, shoe wax and lemon: the smells of my childhood. Val is four, now. Her childhood smells of lab chemicals, frozen dinners and oil paints. Mum, I'm sorry.

I found Dad in the kitchen, peeling potatoes of all things. I'll never know how you manage to wrangle him into kitchen work like you do when we grew up with him swearing it was women's business, girl jobs. You're amazing. A force of nature.

Dad hugged me, congratulated me on my promotion while he handed me an apron and your second best peeler. Hasn't anyone told you yet that the only people who categorise their peelers are washed out, nineteen-fifties housewives?

Mum, I'm sorry.

I'm sorry I'm not everything you ever dreamed of. I'm sorry I'm not Ramona, with her two-point-one children and her white picket fence, her stay-at-home lifestyle and her church-every-Sunday. I'm sorry I followed in Dad's footsteps and forsook yours. I'm sorry my brain wasn't built for cleaning, that I could never find any joy in endless, cyclic, thankless scrubbing. I'm sorry that I find the make of genes more intriguing than the ironing of jeans, that my child knows the taste of frozen carrots and store-bought cheesecake, that I grow my greens on a petri dish instead of a home-dug garden.

I'm sorry, most of all, that this makes you sorry.

Val, at least, can't disappoint you. Although I've already applied to enrol her in the advanced science stream next year when school starts, she loves the kitchen too, loves mixing and brewing and beating. She owns more cooking equipment than I do—she thanks you for the cupcake set, by the way.

What she loves most of all though is art. She'll sit and watch her father for hours at a time. A four year old! Sitting still! It's astounding. I used to have these dreams, when I was pregnant, when we found out we were having a little girl… I used to dream that she'd grow up just like me, practical and unromantic, logical and not at all homey.

And then she grew up, and she loves glitter and sparkles and ponies, loves dress-ups and tiaras and pink. Oh, she's logical, my darling little baby logician who demands why she has to eat her pumpkin when carrots are better for making vitamin A anyway; but she cooks, and she loves to paint.

I know, all children love to play at house, love to get their fingers messy and smear colours across a page. I probably even did. But Mum, how do you bear it? What do you do, that moment when you first realise that this person that was once like a second heart in your own body is now someone distinct, someone different—

Someone *not you*?

Mum, I'm sorry. I'm sorry I wasn't

who you wanted me to be. But most of all I'm sorry that I made that difference so hard. You loved me, every day. I couldn't ask for me.

I love you.

Thank you for everything.

THE MAKING OF *UNDERSTANDING*

Ah, the complications of mother-daughter relationships! You're young, and you think you know everything about the way your mother raised you, and you see everything they did wrong, and everything you think they could have done better… And then you have your own kid, and realise that these things come with no instruction manuals and it's a wonder if anyone makes it unscathed to adulthood, that we all screw up our children somehow, and suddenly, you understand.

Ironically enough, I wrote the first draft of this piece in uni for my creative writing class, long before I was a parent. This story went through many iterations, mostly as I tried to tell it as a straight narrative, before I settled on the letter format and cut the length by over half. It's really more vignette than story, but regardless, may it serve to celebrate—if only for a moment—that we all deserve to have someone on our side who will support us in the life paths we choose.

Read more by Amy Laurens!

April Showers: six rainy autumn stories

CRYSTALLINE AND BRIGHT

I stood, staring down into the teal-blue river water, ignoring the chatter behind my back. Snow covered the ground around me, hiding bumps and ridges, soothing out sharp edges. To my right, the dark stone shadow of the bridge stood like a guardian, watchful, alert. Snow rimmed its edges; every so often some shifted in a sudden breeze and landed in the quiet river below with a gentle splash.

The willows on the far bank slept quietly under their snow blanket, their green sappy smell hidden by the cold, sharp scent of the snow.

Stop.

Start again.

It wasn't actually winter. It was early spring, with the grass green and new, the sound of a lawnmower buzzing in the distance and the scent of cut grass drifting on the wind. Moss covered the shadowed side of the old stone bridge, and willows stretched their fingers to the slow-moving, drowsy little river that bordered the grounds of the school.

A butterfly flittered past, white wings speckled with black like soot.

The world felt fresh, and green, and full of promise.

I was still ignoring the chattering behind me.

Stop.

Start again.

It's summer, and the air is swelteringly hot. Sweat drips down the back of my neck, pools under my arms, under my awkward breasts. The river in front of me is milky-blue, gentle, quiet, and I long to strip off my shirt and jeans and throw myself into the water.

It's not just the breathtakingly sharp cold of the icemelt I'm craving; it's the feeling of being *clean*.

The air stinks of a fish that Lander left out on the bank near the bridge, rotting to pieces in the high temperatures.

I'm still ignoring the chatter.

Stop.

Let's try once more.

It's autumn—of course—and the willows have turned yellow, their little leaves dropping into the milk-water, eddying slowly away from the shadow of the bridge.

Behind me, the emerald lawn of the old school buildings is ringed with gem-toned maples, butter-leafed poplars, silver-and-gold birches. Occasionally, the wind catches stray leaves and flings them into the pond.

I can still hear the voices behind me.

All of these pictures are true, and none of them are.

Not precisely, not uniquely; they're all composites, the merging and piecing together of hundreds of memories of similar experiences, of all the times I stood on the river bank and stared longingly into its depths, imagining myself a naiad with a secret home to return to, somewhere people loved me.

These images have to be composites, because for every time I was down at the river, I was focusing only on two things: ignoring the voices, and watching the water.

All the other details, the little bits of specificity that allow me to recall the place in so much explicit detail? I never noticed them at the time.

And so I have to piece them together, collage-fashion, or else I have nothing to say. Nothing to see.

Nothing except the water, milky-blue that occasionally, in the right light, at the right time of day, flashed teal and came alive.

Keep reading! Head to
www.inkprintpress.com/
amylaurens/aprilshowers/
to buy your copy now!

ABOUT THE AUTHOR

AMY LAURENS is an award-winning Australian author of fantasy fiction for all ages. While she does love JellyBelly jellybeans, she prefers chocolate to lollies (candy) for the most part, and while she definitely hates cleaning, the arts have more of her attention these days than the sciences.

Amy has written the award-winning portal-fantasy *Sanctuary* series (the first book is *Where Shadows Rise*), the humorous fantasy *Kaditeos* series, the young adult series *Storm Foxes*, and a whole host of non-fiction.

You can find out more about her and her books at:

www.AmyLaurens.com

INKLETS

Collect them all! Released on the 1st and 15th of each month.

INKLET #055
Allure
AMY LAURENS

The LIES We KNOW
LIANA BROOKS

INKLET #057
AFTERMATH & Fool Me Once
AMY LAURENS

INKLET #058
Purity
An Age Of Unicorns Story
AMY LAURENS

INKLET #059
Saved
AMY LAURENS

INKLET #060
A Kiss is the Secret
AMY LAURENS

INKLET #061
A Changing Tides Story
Fire Bright
AMY LAURENS

INKLET #062
Hades AND Persephone
LIANA BROOKS

INKLET #063
Just So Long As You're Happy
AMY LAURENS

INKLET #064
Theft Of A Lifetime
LIANA BROOKS

INKLET #065
Shoe
AMY LAURENS

INKLET #066
Published AUTHOR
LIANA BROOKS

DOUBLE ISSUE
INKLET #067
THE REMARKABLE INSIGHT OF JELLYBEANS & Understanding
AMY LAURENS

INKLET #068
Desperate Measures
AMY LAURENS

INKLET #069
Rock-a-bye
LIANA BROOKS

INKLET #070
the Other Carly
AMY LAURENS

INKLET #071
By By Bioluminescent Light
AMY LAURENS

INKLET #072
Even Villains Grant Wishes
A Heroes & Villains Story
LIANA BROOKS